Accidental Genius

Science Puzzles for Clever Kids

DINOSAURS, MAMMOTHS, DODOS, and SABERTOOTHS

Alix Wood

WINDMILL BOOKS

Published in 2023 by Windmill Books,
an Imprint of Rosen Publishing
2544 Clinton St.
Buffalo, NY 14224

Written and designed by Alix Wood

Printed in the United States of America

CPSIA Compliance Information: Batch CWWM23
For Further Information contact Rosen Publishing at 1-800-237-9932

Cataloging-in-Publication Data

Names: Wood, Alix.
Title: Dinosaurs, mammoths, dodos, and sabertooths / Alix Wood.
Description: New York : Windmill Books, 2023. | Series: Accidental genius: science puzzles for clever kids| Includes knowledge test.
Identifiers: ISBN 9781538392461 (pbk) | ISBN 9781538392478 (library bound) | ISBN 9781538392485 (ebook)
Subjects: LCSH: Dinosaurs--Juvenile literature | Dodo--Juvenile literature | Extinct animals--Juvenile literature | Fossils--Juvenile literature | Prehistoric peoples--Juvenile literature | Saber-toothed tigers--Juvenile literature | Woolly mammoth--Juvenile literature
Classification: LCC QE861.5 W66 2023 | DDC 567.9--dc23

Contents

A Planet Is Born

Our planet, Earth, formed about 4.5 billion years ago. At first, it was just a ball of swirling gas and dust! Then it cooled, and formed a rocky crust. Rain began to fall and fill the oceans. Nothing was alive. There was just rock and water.

A few million years later, tiny living things started to appear. How? No one is too sure. Some scientists believe life started in the oceans. Other scientists think living things arrived on rocks flying through space!

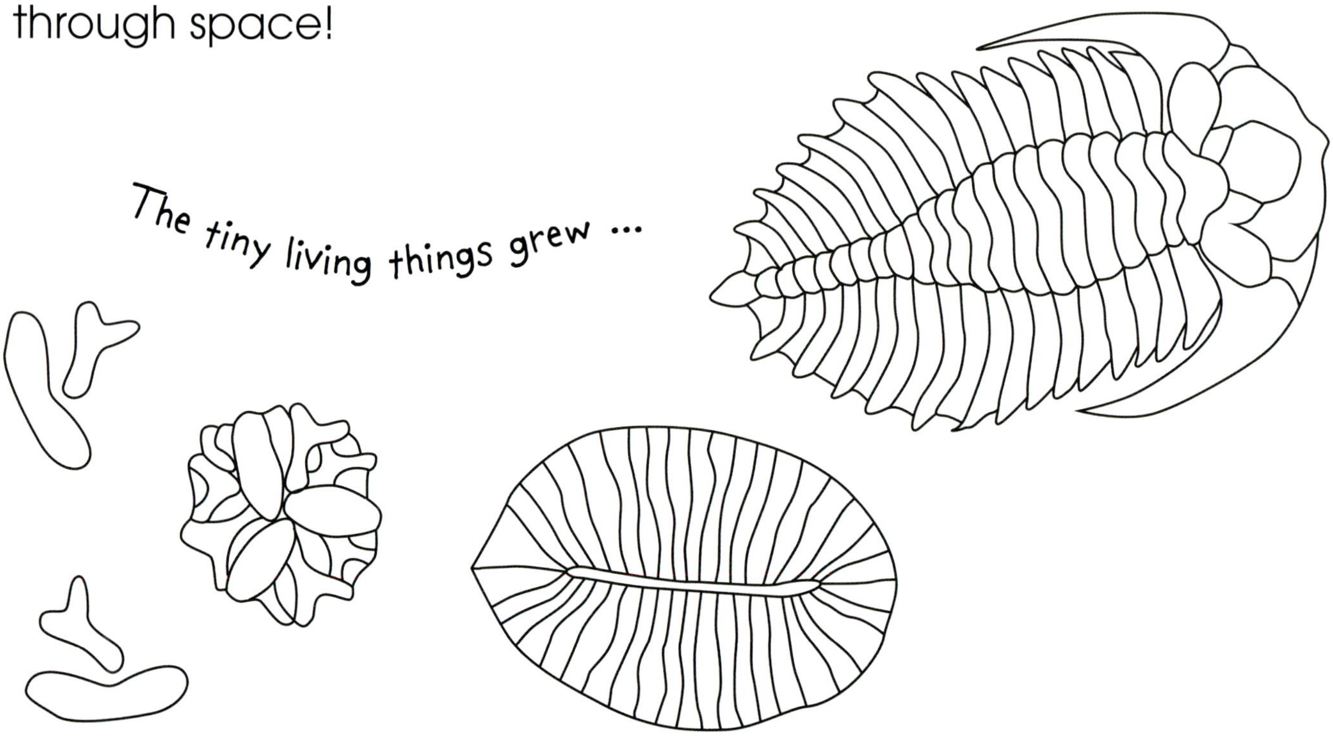

Did you know that Earth is the only planet we know of where plants and animals can live?

Color It In

Ask an adult to make copies of these pages. Then, you can color on the copies!

... and changed ...

... until there were huge dinosaurs stomping around on Earth.

Dinosaur Reptiles

Dinosaurs were a type of reptile. They came in many shapes and sizes. Some could fly, and some could swim. Some had scales, others had feathers. Some were even covered in armor plates!

Reptiles are animals with dry scaly skin that lay soft-shelled eggs on land. Their legs stick out either side of their body, so they waddle as they walk. Crocodiles and lizards are reptiles. A dinosaur is a type of reptile that lived long ago.

a crocodile

Dinosaurs' legs were under their bodies. This let them run much faster than other reptiles.

Use your finger to trace an imaginary line matching each dinosaur or reptile picture to the right description.

1. Allosaurus

Allosaurus was a large meat-eating dinosaur. It walked on two legs. It had a long tail, and sharp claws and teeth.

2. Velociraptor

Velociraptors were about the size of a turkey. They had long claws and feathers, but could not fly. They could run very fast.

3. Pteranodon

Pteranodons were large flying reptiles that lived at the same time as dinosaurs. They had a long crest on the back of their heads.

4. Plesiosaur

Plesiosaurs were reptiles that lived in the ocean. They swam using four flippers. They lived at the same time as the dinosaurs.

All About Fossils

How do we know dinosaurs existed? We have found dinosaur fossils! Fossils are evidence of a plant or animal found in rock. People have found fossils of dinosaur bones, eggs, footprints, and even dinosaur poop!

Scientists who study fossils are called paleontologists.

Fossils form when dead animals and plants fall into thick underwater mud. A type of rock that is created underwater forms in and around the bones.

Scientists can tell a lot from fossils. They can build dinosaur skeletons from the bones, teeth, and claws.

Be a Paleontologist!

Can you see where the missing bones fit in this dinosaur skeleton?

How far apart footprints are can show scientists how fast a dinosaur ran! Try it. Wet the bottom of your shoes and walk along a dry sidewalk. Wet your shoes again and run next to your walking footprints. Can you see the difference?

Dinosaur Days

Dinosaurs lived from about 245 million years ago to 65.5 million years ago. That's a long time! Scientists split that time into periods. Dinosaurs lived during the Triassic, Jurassic, and Cretaceous periods. Not all dinosaurs lived at the same time.

Shape Match

Look at the time line at the bottom of these pages. Then use your finger to draw an imaginary line to match each shape to the correct time period.

Paleozoic Era

Jurassic Period

Triassic Period

Cretaceous Period

Paleozoic Era | Triassic Period

251 million years ago (mya)

200 mya

Dino Sudoku

Each red square, row, and column must have a creature from each time period. Can you find the missing ones?

Did you know ammonites lived from the Paleozoic Era all the way to the end of the Cretaceous Period?

Jurassic Period

146 mya

Cretaceous Period

65 mya

Moving Land

Millions of years ago, the land on Earth didn't look like it does now. Instead of seven separate continents, there was one big area of land, surrounded by a single ocean. Very slowly, the land broke apart.

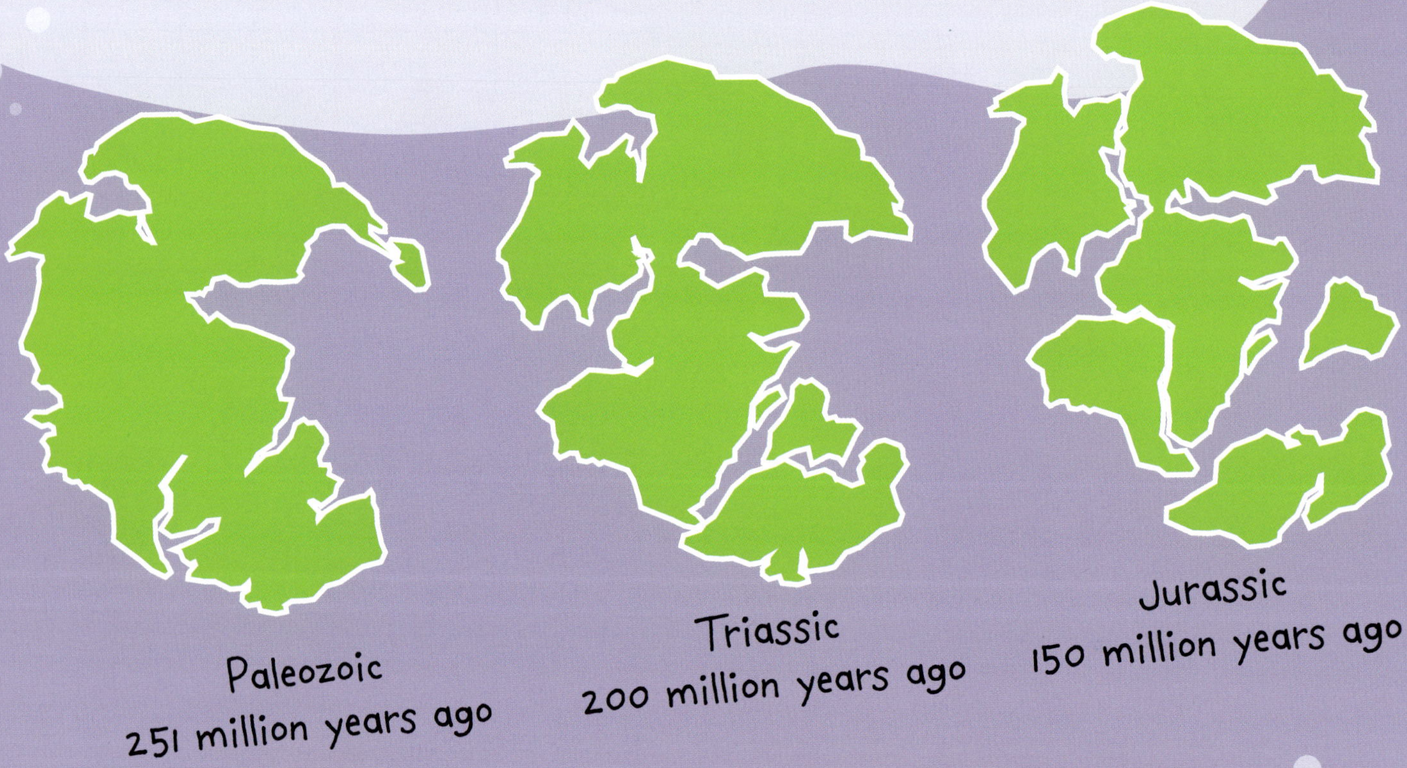

The continents are always slowly moving. Right now, Australia is heading toward Asia. Africa is moving away from Asia. North and South America are drifting West!

When the dinosaurs died out, North America, Europe, and Asia were still joined together! Australia was still joined to Antarctica, too.

Present day

Cretaceous
65 million years ago

Color In the 7 Continents

Ask an adult to make a copy of this page. Then, you can color on the copy!

Flying Beasts

Flying reptiles, known as pterosaurs, lived at the same time as the dinosaurs. The *Pterodactylus* is probably the best-known pterosaur.

Do You Know Your Pterosaurs?

Finish these sentences with the right word. Write your answers on a separate sheet of paper.

1. Most pterosaur wings were made of
   a) skin   b) feathers

2. Pterosaurs laid   -shelled eggs
   a) hard   b) soft

3. Pterosaurs were
   a) dinosaurs   b) reptiles

Scary Meat Eaters

The meat-eating dinosaurs were a type of dinosaur known as theropods. The huge *Tyrannosaurus rex* was a theropod. Theropods could be very small, too. *Compsognathus* was the size of a chicken! Theropods walked on two feet. Their arms were small, with two or three claws.

Tyrannosaurus rex (*T. rex*) was the size of a school bus. It had powerful jaws and 60 razor-sharp teeth.

Color It In

Ask an adult to make a copy of this picture or you can trace it. Then, you can color on the copy!

Theropod Hunt

Can you find:

1. *Allosaurus* 
2. *T. rex* 
3. *Spinosaurus* 
4. *Gallimimus* 

Modern birds are related to theropods. Like birds, theropods had hollow bones, and birdlike feet!

Dinosaur Eggs

Most types of dinosaur laid eggs. They could be very large. One fossil of a dinosaur egg found in China was over 2 feet (60 cm) long! Most dinosaurs laid around 20 eggs at a time. Laying a lot of eggs meant some might survive if the nest was raided by predators.

Inside a Dinosaur Egg

The egg has everything a baby dinosaur will need. The yolk provides food. A waste sac collects any poop. The leathery shell protects the embryo. An air sac gives the baby some air as it tries to hatch, too.

Egg Hatch

1 2 3 4

Our pictures of a dinosaur hatching have gotten mixed up. Can you put the pictures in the right order? Number them starting from 1 up to 4, writing your answers on a separate sheet of paper.

a

b
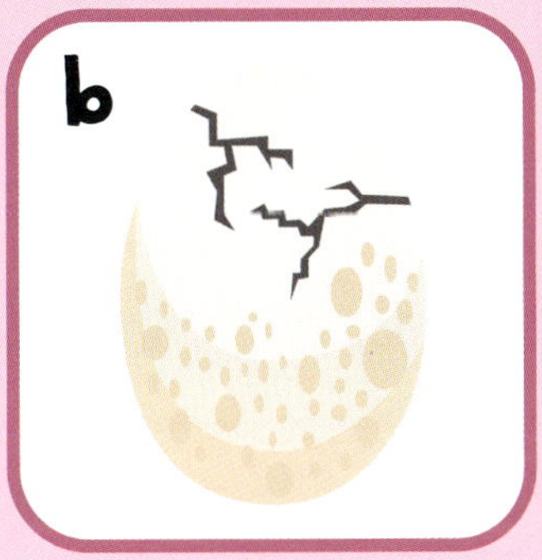

c
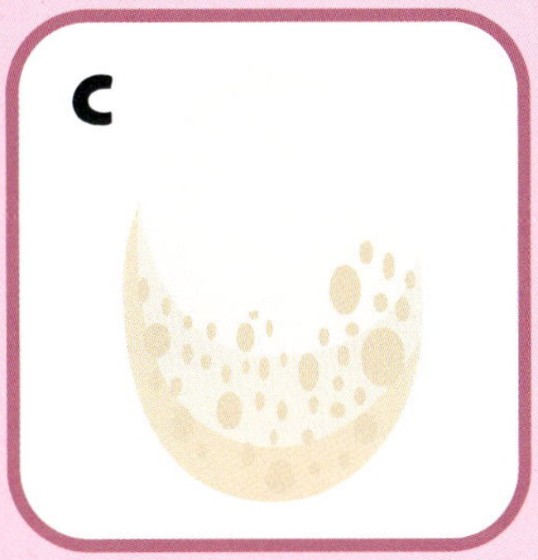

d

Hatch a Fizzy Dinosaur Egg

You will need: 1 cup of baking soda, small plastic dinosaur toy, large bowl, 1/4 cup of water, vinegar, baking sheet

1. Slowly add the water to the baking soda to form a dough ball.
2. Flatten the dough ball. Place a toy dinosaur in the center. Wrap the dough around the toy to form an egg shape.
3. Let the eggs dry on the baking sheet overnight.
4. To hatch your dinosaur, slowly pour vinegar over the egg. The reaction between the vinegar and the baking soda will cause the egg to fizz and dissolve!

Spots, Scales, Feathers?

Fossils of dinosaur bones, claws, and teeth help us build their skeletons. Fossilized footprints and skin prints can show scales or feathers, too. But we can really only guess what color they were!

Design Your Own Dinosaur

Did this dinosaur have feathers, scales, wings, or spines? What color was it? Have fun designing your own dinosaur.

Make a copy or trace a copy of this dinosaur on a separate sheet of paper. Then, create your own dino design!

Some dinosaurs had to hide to survive. Having the same color as your surroundings is called "camouflage." Scientists think dinosaurs living near rocks were probably gray or brown. Forest dinosaurs were probably green.

Bright dinosaurs would find it easier to find a mate. So, some dinosaurs might have been bright red or yellow!

Can you spot 5 camouflaged dinosaurs hiding in this picture?

Terrifying Tails

Ankylosaurs were short, wide, slow, four-legged dinosaurs. They ate plants. They lived at the same time as big, scary, meat-eating dinosaurs. To protect themselves, they were covered in armor-like plates. They also had a secret weapon!

On the end of their tail they had a club that they could swing at an enemy.

Stegosaurus was another slow-moving plant eater.

It had spikes on its tail! It used them as a weapon, and to slash through the undergrowth to find food.

Join the Dots

What has this *Stegosaurus* got on its back? Trace the dots with your finger to find out!

Word Search

B	E	A	K	Z	O	S	Y	H	E
L	F	P	N	S	G	B	U	L	C
E	S	A	R	N	C	X	R	O	R
P	F	E	A	T	H	E	R	S	E
H	S	P	T	N	W	O	I	U	S
O	D	C	R	M	P	I	H	R	T
R	C	L	A	W	S	T	N	T	S
N	W	I	M	L	P	N	K	G	B
B	S	P	I	N	E	S	U	I	S
U	L	Q	U	T	V	S	E	R	S

Find the nine words below that describe some dinosaur parts.

FEATHERS
CREST
SCALES
CLAWS
BEAK
CLUB
WINGS
SPINES
HORN

Very Big, VerySpeedy

If a dinosaur wasn't covered in armor, or didn't have a club for a tail, how did it protect itself from the scary meat eaters? It had to be either VERY big, or super fast!

Ornithomimus dug its toes into the ground when it ran.

Height: 16 feet (5 m)
Weight: 330 pounds (150 kg)
Speed: 40 miles per hour (64 kph)

Argentinosaurus is one of the largest creatures ever to walk the Earth.

Length: 130 ft (40 m)
Weight: 110 tons (100 tonnes)
Speed: a very slow 4 miles per hour (6.4 kph)

Compsognathus was the size of a chicken.

Length: 3 feet (0.9 m)
Weight: 12 pounds (5.4 kg)
Speed: 40 miles per hour (64 kph)

Velociraptor liked to eat leftovers.

Length: 6 feet (1.8 m)
Weight: 55 pounds (25 kg)
Speed: 25 miles per hour (40.2 kph)

Dinosaur Names

Scientists use Greek or Latin words to name dinosaurs.

saurus = lizard
veloci = fast
raptor = thief
ornitho = birdlike

mimus = mimic
compso = pretty
gnathus = jaw

Dinosaurs can be named after the location they were found, or the person who found them. Can you guess where Argentinosaurus was discovered?

Word Scramble

Unscramble the first part of these dinosaur names to find the speedy dinosaurs. Write your answers on a separate sheet of paper.

1) I V O L C E — _ _ _ _ _ _ RAPTOR

2) I N O R O H T — _ _ _ _ _ _ _ MIMUS

3) O P C O M S — _ _ _ _ _ _ GNATHUS

Dinosaur Horns

Triceratops was a plant-eating dinosaur. It was as heavy as a truck! *Triceratops* means three-horned face. Their larger horns could be 3 feet (1 m) long!

Color It In

Ask an adult to make a copy of this picture or you can trace it. Then, you can color on the copy!

Triceratops

Triceratops fought other dinosaurs using their horns.

Their necks were protected with a bony frill.

They had a sharp, parrot-like beak.

They had thick skin and strong legs.

Spot the Difference

Can you find 7 differences between these two pictures of a dinosaur museum?

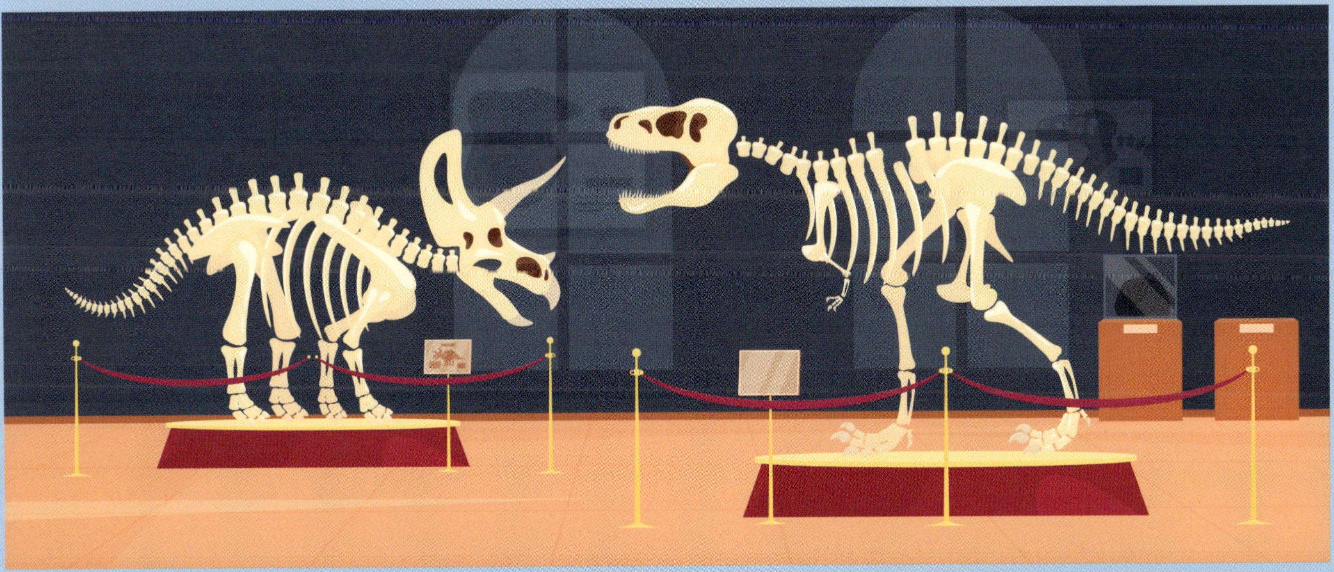

Can you guess which two dinosaurs these skeletons might belong to? Write your answer on a separate sheet of paper.

1. _ . _ E _

2. _ _ _ C E R A _ _ _ _

Who Eats Who?

All living things need food. Plants get their energy from sunlight, water, and soil. Many dinosaurs ate plants. But meat-eating dinosaurs needed plants, too. Why? Because they ate the plant-eaters!

A dinosaur food chain

Can you work out what's missing from this dinosaur food chain?

Make a "Dinosaur World" Fossil

Dead plants and dinosaurs can leave prints in the ground where they lay. Over millions of years the mold might fill with minerals. This creates a cast of the fossil. Try it.

You will need: deep, large rectangle of modeling clay, small plastic dinosaur, leaves, plaster of Paris, an adult to help you

1. Press a toy dinosaur and some leaves into a thick rectangle of modeling clay. Carefully lift them out again. You have made a fossil mold.

2. Ask an adult to help fill the mold with plaster of Paris. Once the plaster has dried, remove the fossil. This is a fossil cast.

Where Did the Dinosaurs Go?

Dinosaurs are extinct. Extinct means they no longer exist. The last dinosaurs died out about 65.5 million years ago. Scientists have a few different ideas about why this happened.

Some scientists think a large asteroid hit Earth and created a huge dust cloud. The dust blocked out the sun. Plants couldn't grow. Having no plants destroyed the dinosaur food chain.

Other scientists think Earth got too hot, or too cold, for the dinosaurs.

Asteroid Strike

Which asteroid is heading for Earth?

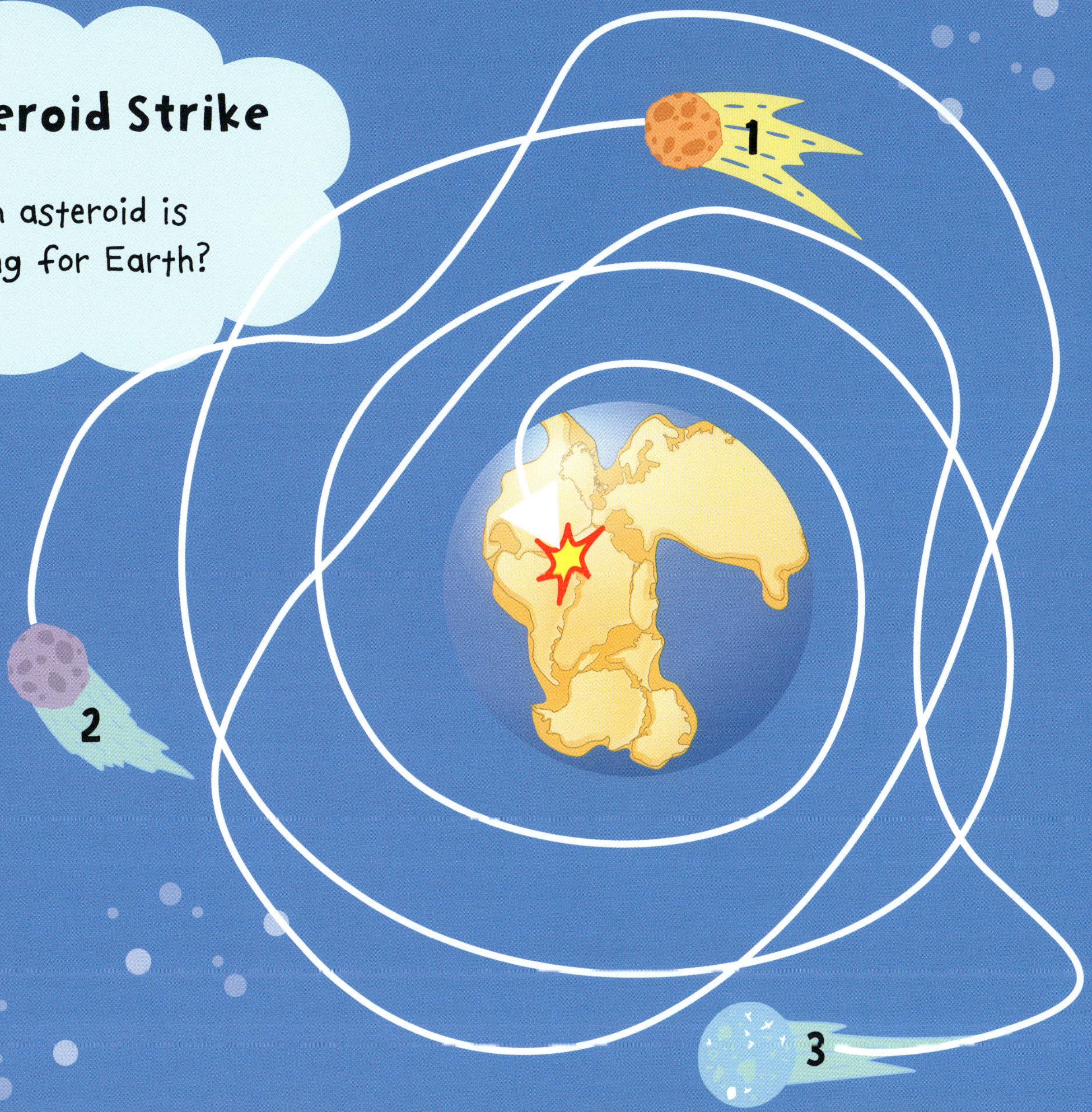

Survivors

Some animals survived whatever caused the death of the dinosaurs. Scientists do not know why they lived but the dinosaurs did not. Early types of frogs, birds, turtles, lizards, and snakes found a way to survive. That is why we have them today.

Did you know? Modern birds came from therapods, not the flying pterosaurs! *T. rex* was a therapod!

The Dodo Bird

The last time anyone saw a dodo was in 1662. Dodos were around 3 feet (1 m) tall. They couldn't fly. They didn't need to. Nothing hunted them on their island of Mauritius.

Why did they disappear? When people arrived, they hunted them. Animals the people brought with them ate their eggs. Dodos laid just one egg, on the ground!

Trace the dots with your finger or trace them on a photocopy to see what a dodo looked like.

Which color dodo can reach the nest? Trace their path with your finger to find out!

Woolly Mammoths

Earth goes through periods when it is very hot, or very cold. About 20,000 years ago, there was an ice age. A huge type of hairy elephant called a mammoth lived during the ice age.

Mammoths were about the size of an African elephant.

Mammoths had small ears. Elephants lose heat through their ears, so small ears helped them keep warm.

Their enormous tusks helped them dig in the snow for plants to eat.

Humans lived at the same time as mammoths.

Mammoths were covered in two layers of thick fur.

Polar Bear

I am covered in thick fur that helps me hide in the snow.

Giraffe

Dark patterns on my skin help keep me cool.

Crocodile

I like to be in the sun. I open my mouth if I need to cool off.

Match the animals that need cold weather or hot weather.

Seal

I have a thick layer of fat to keep me warm in the ocean.

Emperor Penguins

We huddle together to keep warm.

African Elephant

My big ears help keep me cool.

Ice Ages

Scientists believe our planet has had at least five major ice ages. We are living in an ice age now. This ice age started 2.5 million years ago.

Earth should be a lot cooler than it is right now, but global warming is causing Earth to warm up too quickly. Global warming is when gases trap heat around Earth. The gas comes from burning coal, wood, and oil.

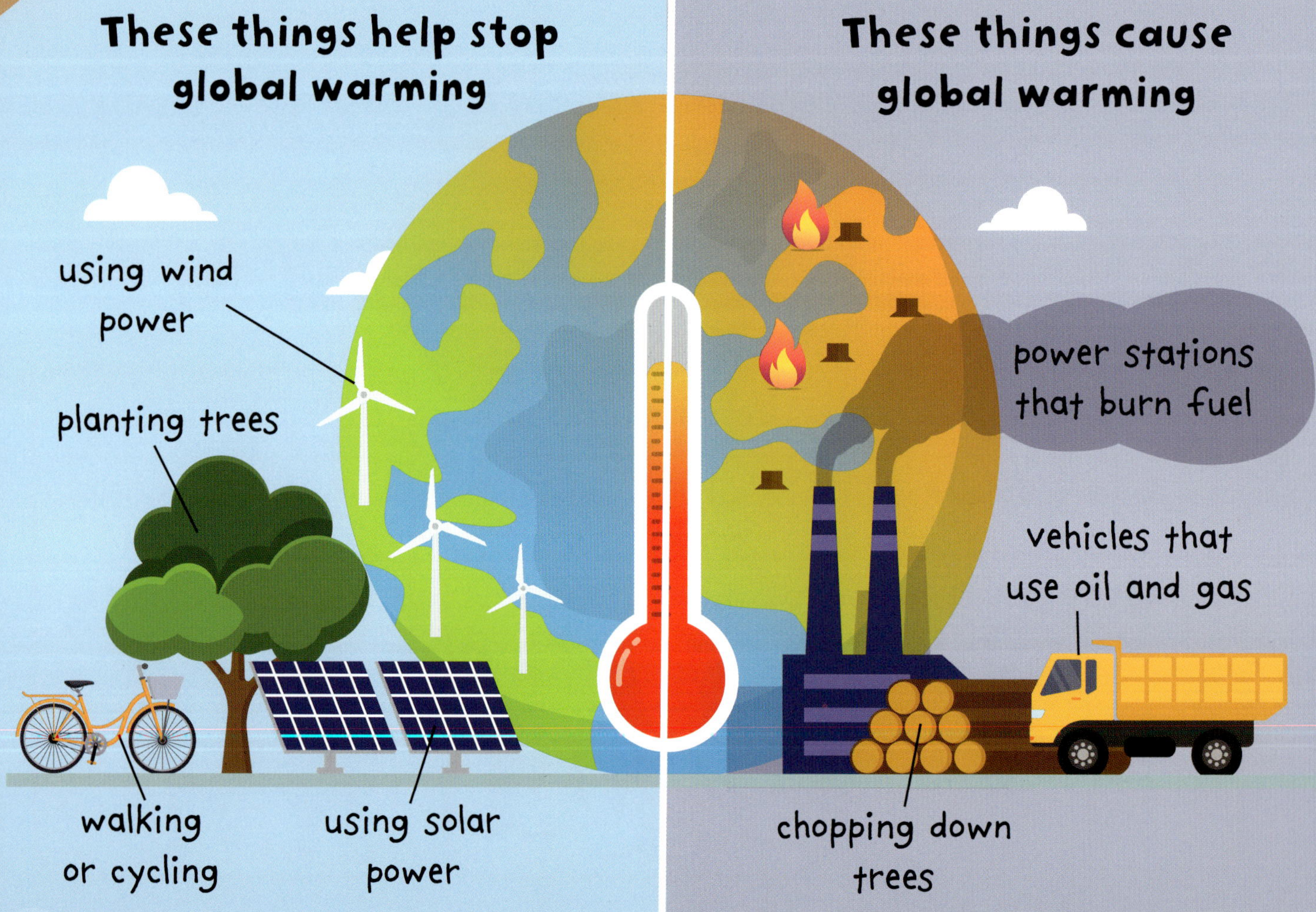

Quiz Time!

1. Can you help stop global warming by planting a tree?
   a) yes   b) no

2. Can driving a gas-powered truck cause global warming?
   a) yes   b) no

Check the box if it helps stop global warming. ✓

Put an X in the box if it causes global warming. ✗

Remember – cover the picture with tracing paper first if you are sharing this book.

Color It In

Ask an adult to make a copy of this picture or you can trace it. Then, you can color on the copy!

Sabertooth Cats

Smilodon was a big, sabertooth cat. It had two long, sawlike teeth. It had huge paws with long, razor-sharp claws!

Its jaw could open more than 120 degrees! That's twice as wide as a modern big cat.

Some scientists think *Smilodon* hunted in packs. Why? Fossils of healed broken bones have been found. The injured cat may have been fed by others in the pack.

Shadow Match

Smilodon is hunting at dusk. Can you match the shadow to the right animal?

Titanis   Woolly Mammoth   Woolly Rhinoceros

Word Search

Find these 8 animals that lived in *Smilodon*'s era.

B	E	M	A	M	M	O	T	H	E
L	F	P	A	S	E	B	U	C	W
E	S	A	R	S	C	X	R	A	R
P	F	E	R	T	T	E	R	M	L
N	S	O	T	N	T	O	I	E	S
O	H	C	R	O	D	I	D	L	T
S	C	S	Y	I	E	O	P	O	F
I	W	O	M	L	E	N	K	P	N
B	C	P	I	N	R	S	U	S	S
U	L	S	M	I	L	O	D	O	N

MAMMOTH
MASTODON
BISON
CAMELOPS
HORSE
SMILODON
DEER
COYOTE

Early Humans

Scientists have evidence that the earliest humans came from Africa. Since many tools early humans created were made out of stone, this period is called the Stone Age.

Humans did not live at the same time as dinosaurs. Dinosaurs died out 63 million years before! They did live at the same time as sabertooth cats and woolly mammoths. Can you spot them?

Early man sometimes drew animals on their cave walls using a charred stick. Can you match these drawings to the animal name?

1

2

3

4

deer | bison | mammoth | horse

What animals would you draw to decorate your cave? Try it on a separate sheet of paper or trace imaginary lines here with your finger.

Use a sheet of paper if you are sharing this book.

Fossil Hunting

The best place to find fossils is your local museum. You can look at the exhibits, and ask the experts where you could look for fossils. If you decide to go fossil hunting, always take a trusted adult with you.

It is easy to spoil a fossil by digging it up badly. If you find a fossil, tell an expert where it is. They might let you help dig it up!

Create a Stay-at-home Fossil Hunt

You will need: a deep bowl, small plastic dinosaurs, sand, soil, a spoon, a paintbrush, scrap paper and pen

1. Place a layer of soil in the bowl. Press a dinosaur into the soil. Write a pretend date on a scrap of paper and bury it with the dinosaur.

2. Cover the dinosaur with a thick layer of sand. Press another dinosaur into that layer, with a later date. Repeat with layers of soil, then sand, until you reach the top of the bowl.

3. Now dig up and date each fossil. Carefully brush or spoon away the sand or soil. The deepest fossils should be the oldest.

Do this activity outside. It can get messy!

Find the Hidden Fossil

Copy the drawing in each square onto a grid that looks like the one below. What fossil did you draw?

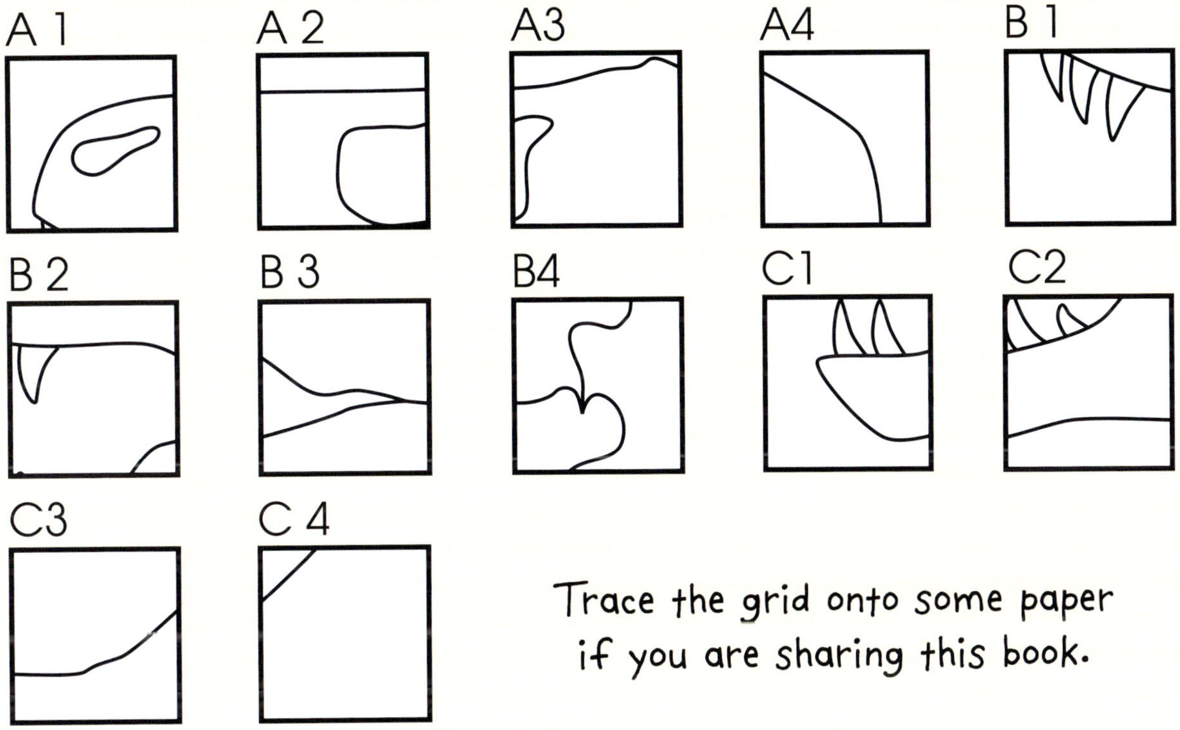

Trace the grid onto some paper if you are sharing this book.

We have filled in the first square for you.

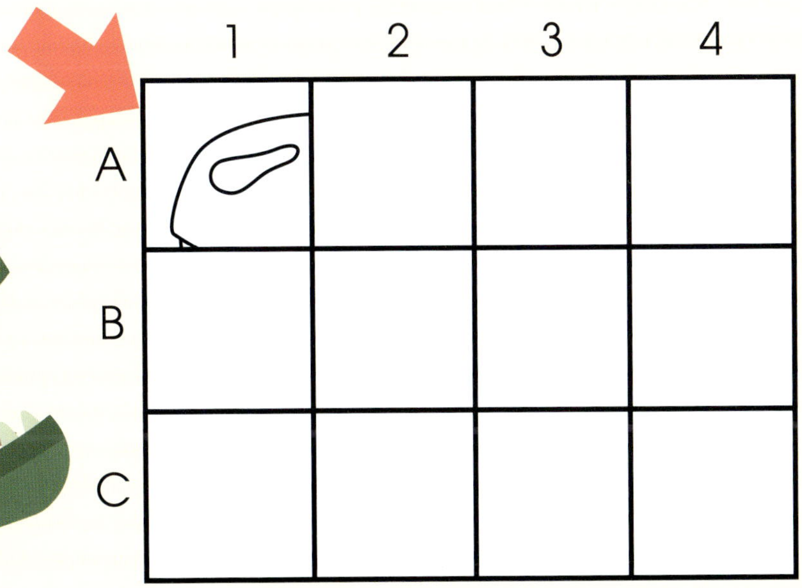

Color It In

Dinosaur Genius Test

Are you a prehistoric genius? Answer these dinosaur questions to find out. You can write your answers on a separate sheet of paper.

1 How can scientists tell how fast a dinosaur ran?

a) They guess.

b) They study fossils of their footprints, to see how far apart they are.

c) They find photographs of dinosaurs running.

2 Why did meat-eating dinosaurs need plants to survive?

a) They built houses out of them.

b) They ate them.

c) They ate the plant-eating dinosaurs.

3 What color would camouflage a dinosaur in the forest?

a) green b) blue c) red

4 How did woolly mammoths keep warm in the ice age?

a) Having small ears helped them not lose heat.

b) They had two layers of thick fur.

c) Both a and b.

5 Were humans alive at the same time as dinosaurs?

a) yes b) no

Answers

Page 7: 1) a 2) c 3) d 4) b

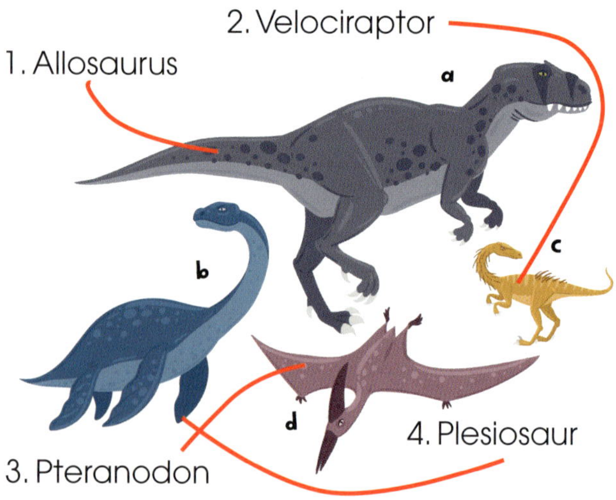

page 9: 1) b 2) c 3) d 4) a

Page 10:

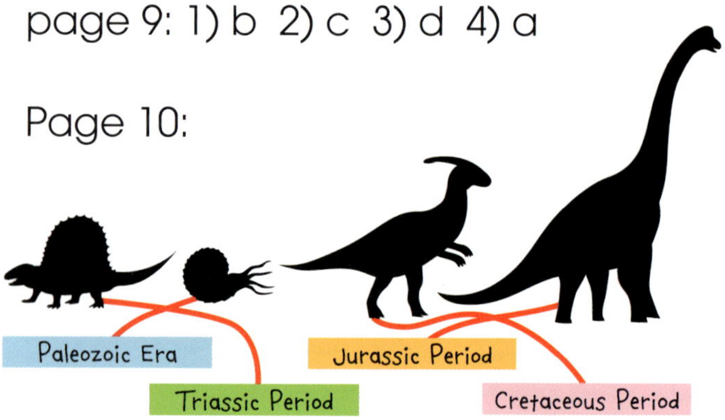

Page 11: 1) b 2) a 3) c 4) d

Page 15:

1 a: Most pterosaur wings were made of skin

2 b: Pterosaurs laid soft-shelled eggs

3 b: Pterosaurs were reptiles

Page 17:

Page 19: c = 1, b = 2, d = 3, a = 4

Page 21:

Page 23: Join the dots.
A stegosaurus has two rows of plates along its back.

Page 23:

B	E	A	K	Z	O	S	Y	H	E
L	F	P	N	S	G	B	U	L	C
E	S	A	R	N	C	X	R	O	R
P	F	E	A	T	H	E	R	S	E
H	S	P	T	N	W	O	I	U	S
O	D	C	R	M	P	I	H	R	T
R	C	L	A	W	S	T	N	T	S
N	W	I	M	L	P	N	K	G	B
B	S	P	I	N	E	S	U	I	S
U	L	Q	U	T	V	S	E	R	S

Page 25 top: Argentinosaurus was found in Argentina.

Page 25: Word Scramble
1) VELOCI raptor
2) ORNITHO mimus
3) COMPSO gnathus

Page 27:

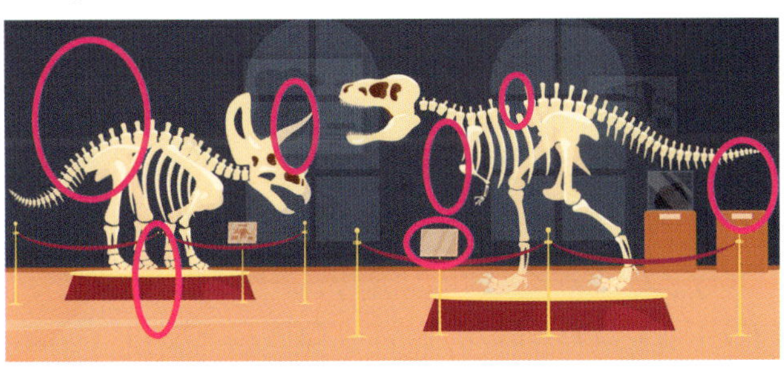

The skeletons were:
1) T. rex
2) Triceratops

Page 29: The plant was missing from the food chain.

Page 31: 1. Asteroid 1 will hit Earth.

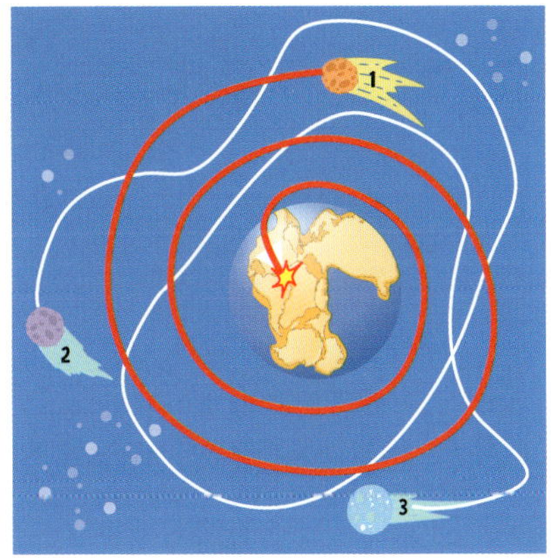

Page 32:

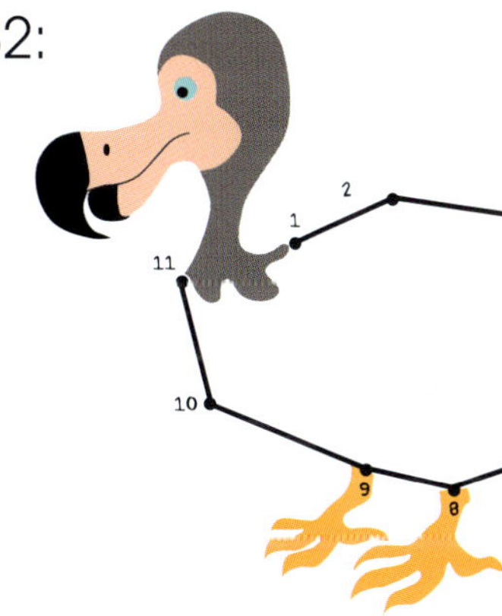

Page 33: The gray dodo reaches the nest.

Page 35:

polar bear	giraffe
seal	crocodile
Emperor penguins	African elephant

Page 37: Quiz

1. a) Yes, you can help stop global warming by planting a tree.

2. a) Yes, driving a gas-powered truck can cause global warming

Page 37: Check the box for the tree, the solar panels, and wind turbine. X the box for the gas-powered car and the factory.

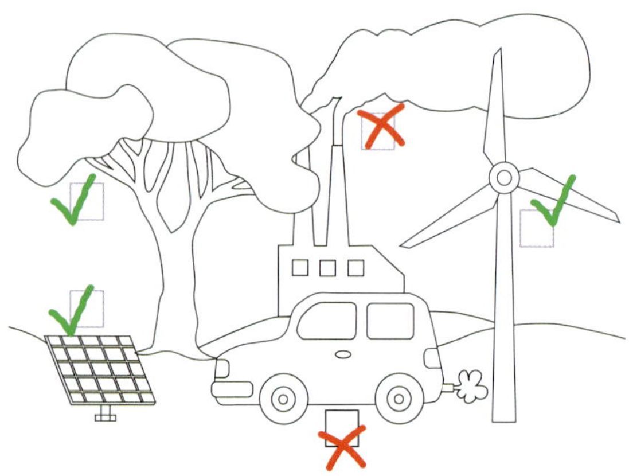

Page 39: a) Woolly mammoth b) Woolly rhinoceros, c) Titanis

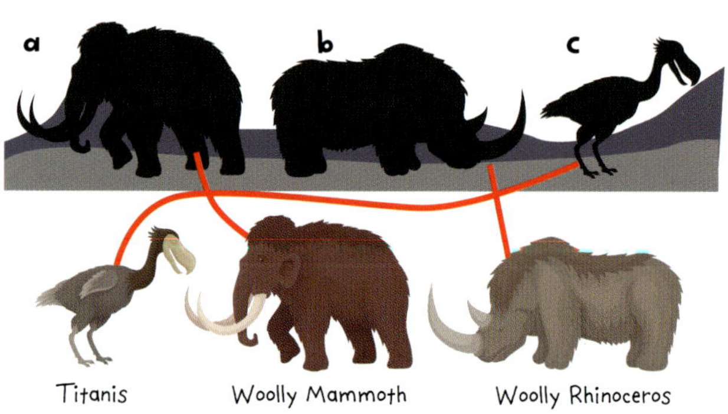

Page 39:

B	E	M	A	M	M	O	T	H	E
L	F	P	A	S	E	B	U	C	W
E	S	A	R	S	C	X	R	A	R
P	F	E	R	T	T	E	R	M	L
N	S	O	T	N	T	O	I	E	S
O	H	C	R	O	D	I	D	L	T
S	C	S	Y	I	E	O	P	O	F
	W	O	M	L	E	N	K	P	N
B	C	P	I	N	R	S	U	S	S
U	L	S	M	I	L	O	D	O	N

Page 40:

Page 41: 1) mammoth 2) deer 3) horse 4) bison

Page 43: You drew a T. rex skull.

Page 44: 1) b - They study fossils of their footprints, to see how far apart they are. 2) c - They ate plant-eating dinosaurs. 3) a - green 4) c - Both a and b. 5) No, humans were not alive at the same time as dinosaurs.